The Key Cutter's Grandson

Chris Bell
Cheryl Orsini

The Key Cutter's Grandson

Fast Forward
Gold Level 22

Text: Chris Bell
Illustrations: Cheryl Orsini
Editor: Cameron Macintosh
Design: Karen Mayo
Series design: James Lowe
Production controller: Seona Galbally
Audio recordings: Juliet Hill, Picture Start
Spoken by: Matthew King and Abbe Holmes

Acknowledgements
For Bruce, Matt, Sal and Dan for encouragement and faith to turn China – briefly – into my reality.

ISBN 978 0 17 012685 4
ISBN 978 0 17 012681 6 (set)

Cengage Learning Australia
Level 7, 80 Dorcas Street
South Melbourne, Victoria Australia 3205
Phone: 1300 790 853

Cengage Learning New Zealand
Unit 4B Rosedale Office Park
331 Rosedale Road, Albany, North Shore NZ 0632
Phone: 0508 635 766

For learning solutions, visit cengage.com.au

Printed in China by 1010 Printing International Ltd
2 3 4 5 6 7 8 12 11 10 09 08

Evaluated in independent research by staff from the Department of Language, Literacy and Arts Education at the University of Melbourne.

The Key Cutter's Grandson

Chris Bell
Cheryl Orsini

Contents

Chapter 1

Finders Keepers

Lei pushed his bag back
onto his shoulder.
How could he watch where he walked
when his bag kept falling off?
"Ouch," he yelled, tripping again
on the broken path.
His bag burst open and books spilled
over the pavement.

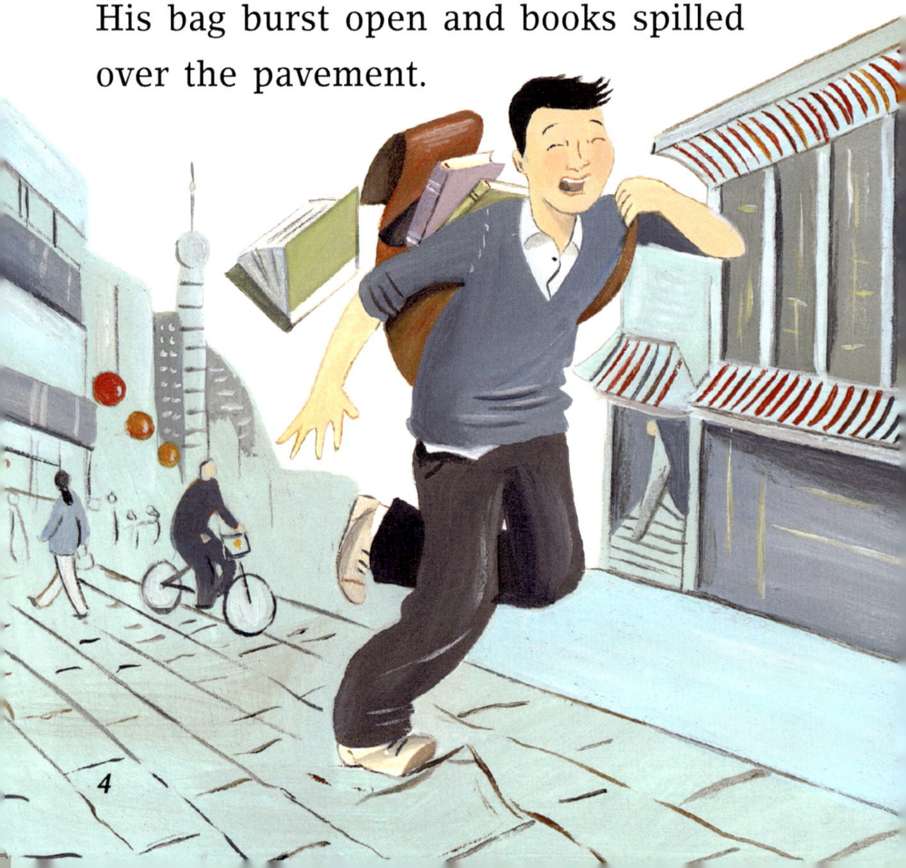

Lei muttered crossly as he bent
to pick them up.
Then he saw a piece
of red and white paper
caught under a loose stone.
Could that be ...?

"Yes," gasped Lei,
glancing around quickly.

The lunchtime crowds walked on,
without looking at him.
Lei pretended he was picking up
his books, then he reached across
and snatched the paper
from under the stone.
He scrunched it in his hand
and began to run.
He didn't stop until he fell, gasping,
through the doorway
of his grandfather's shop.

"What's wrong with you?"
shouted the old key cutter.

Lei shook his head.
"Nothing, Grandfather," he said.

Lei ran to the tiny kitchen
behind the shop
and climbed the narrow stairs
to the space above,
where his mother slept.
He opened his hand.
Crushed under his fingers
lay a 100-yuan note.
Lei had never held so much money
in his life.
He could hardly breathe
for excitement.
Imagine all the things I can buy,
he thought.

Running Words 204

"Lei, come and help me,"
shouted Grandfather, from below.

Quickly, Lei folded the money
into a small square,
pushed it inside an old sock
and stuffed it behind a broken board.
Even the icy cold
would not bother him tonight.
He had many things to think about –
all the things he could buy
with 100 yuan.

Much to Think About

That night, Lei was lying on
his bamboo cot
in the middle of Grandfather's shop.
Nearby, he could hear
Grandfather snoring.
Lei huddled under his bedding.

Usually, he didn't like winter nights
because the cold damp crept up
through the concrete floor.
Tonight, he grinned in the dark.
He was rich.
How many days did Grandfather
have to strain his eyes cutting keys
to make 100 yuan?
Then Lei frowned.

Grandfather's eyes were always red now.
His glasses were old and cracked, but he refused to buy new ones.
"These glasses are good enough," he said.

Lei shook his head.
When he grew up, he would be rich.
He would buy Grandfather new glasses for every day of the week.

The next morning,
Lei walked to school slowly,
stopping to look in every shop window.
Then he saw them – shiny, new shoes
with long white laces.
Lei looked down to see his red sock
peeping out through a hole
in the toe of his shoe.

A man on a bicycle swerved past him.
“Look out,” he yelled.

Lei laughed.
He could buy his own bicycle
with so much money.
So many choices!
Lei decided that he should wait
until he thought of just the right thing
to buy.

Trouble

When Lei walked home for lunch,
he heard a lot of noise ahead
in the street.
There was a crowd on the pavement
outside Grandfather's shop.

"This key does not work," shouted a lady.

Grandfather stared down his nose, where his glasses had slipped. "You are not turning it properly," he said.

The woman shook her head angrily.
"No," she replied.
"I tell you, this key does not work.
It will not turn this way or that way."

Behind him, Lei heard a man
say that the same thing happened
to the key he bought here last week.

Lei watched Grandfather
reach into his pocket,
take out three yuan notes
and hand them to the lady.
She took the notes
and hurried away, saying,
"The old man cannot cut good keys
any more."

Lei's eyes widened in shock.
Of course Grandfather cut good keys.
He was the best key cutter
in all of Fuzhou.

The crowd moved away,
but Lei stood on the street
for a long time.
He watched Grandfather take off
his glasses and rub his red eyes.

For the first time, Lei was scared.
Everyone called Grandfather
the old key cutter,
but, until that moment, Lei had never
thought of Grandfather as old.

Chapter 4

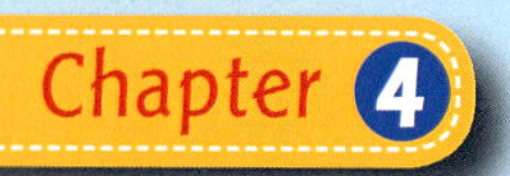

A Hard Choice

Lei walked inside the shop slowly.
He knew he wouldn't be thinking happy thoughts tonight.
Instead he tossed and turned in his bed.
He knew Grandfather didn't sleep well either.
His snores were silent on this night.

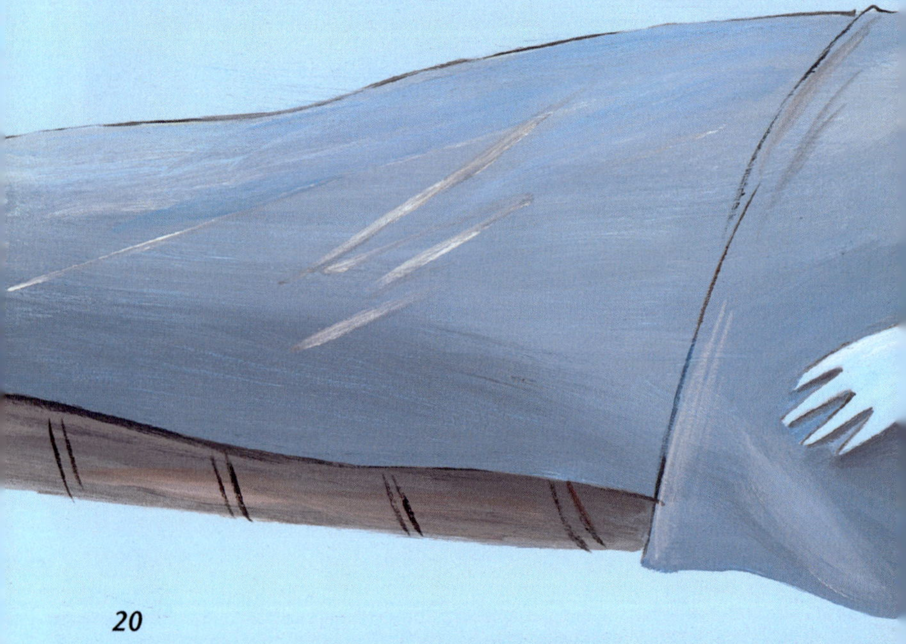

The next morning, Lei waited.
No customers came
to Grandfather's shop
to have new keys cut.

At lunchtime, Lei crept upstairs.
He pulled away the broken board
and tugged out the old sock.
He would give the money
to Grandfather.

At first, Grandfather refused
to take the money.
But when night came and there were
still no customers,
Grandfather and Lei walked together
to the glasses shop.
Grandfather tried on a pair
of new glasses.
"I look good, hey, Grandson?" he asked.

Lei smiled back.
He had not seen his grandfather
look so young for a long time.

On the way home,
Grandfather shook Lei's hand.
"Thank you, Grandson," he said.

Lei felt some crumpled paper
in his hand.
He looked down to see
a ten-yuan note peeping out
from between his fingers.
He knew tonight he would not
feel cold.
He had many things to think about.